Good-Night,  Owl!

FOR MORGAN'S GRANDPA

PAT HUTCHINS

NIGHT

The Bodley Head · London

Copyright © 1972 Pat Hutchins   ISBN 0 370 02016 2   Printed in Great Britain for
The Bodley Head Ltd, 32 Bedford Square, London WC1B 3SG by Cambus Litho, East Kilbride
Published in New York by the Macmillan Company, 1972
First published in Great Britain 1973   Reprinted 1974, 1977, 1979, 1982, 1984, 1986, 1989

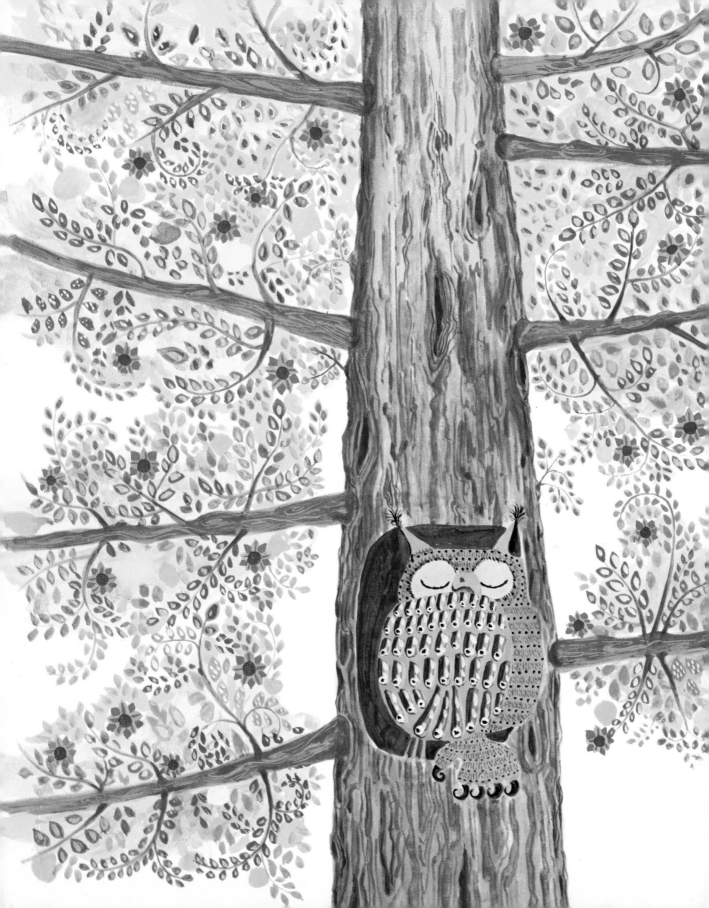

Owl tried to sleep.

The bees buzzed,
buzz buzz,
and Owl tried to sleep.

The squirrel cracked nuts,
crunch crunch,
and Owl tried to sleep.

The crows croaked,
caw caw,
and Owl tried to sleep.

The woodpecker pecked,
rat-a-tat! rat-a-tat!
and Owl tried to sleep.

The starlings chittered,
twit-twit, twit-twit,
and Owl tried to sleep.

The jays screamed,
        ark ark,
and Owl tried to sleep.

The cuckoo called,
cuckoo cuckoo,
and Owl tried to sleep.

The robin peeped,
pip pip,
and Owl tried to sleep.

The sparrows chirped,
cheep cheep,
and Owl tried to sleep.

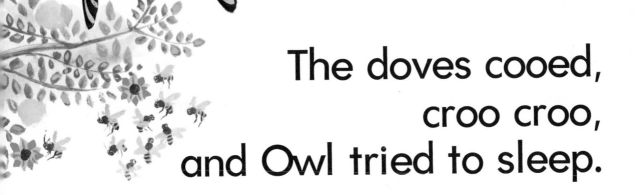

The doves cooed,
croo croo,
and Owl tried to sleep.

The bees buzzed, buzz buzz.
The squirrel cracked nuts,
crunch crunch.
The crows croaked, caw caw.
The woodpecker pecked,
rat-a-tat! rat-a-tat!
The starlings chittered,
twit-twit, twit-twit.
The jays screamed, ark ark.
The cuckoo called,
cuckoo cuckoo.
The robin peeped, pip pip.
The sparrows chirped,
cheep cheep.
The doves cooed, croo croo,
and Owl couldn't sleep.

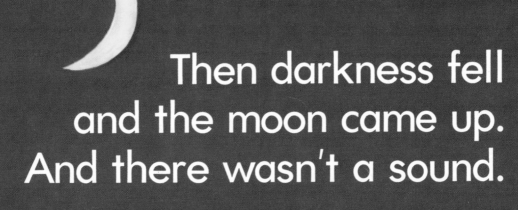

Then darkness fell
and the moon came up.
And there wasn't a sound.

Owl screeched,
screech screech,
and woke everyone up.